Right on!

I'm
ON
It!

by
Andrea
Tsurumi

An **ELEPHANT & PIGGIE LIKE READING!** Book

Hyperion Books for Children / *New York*

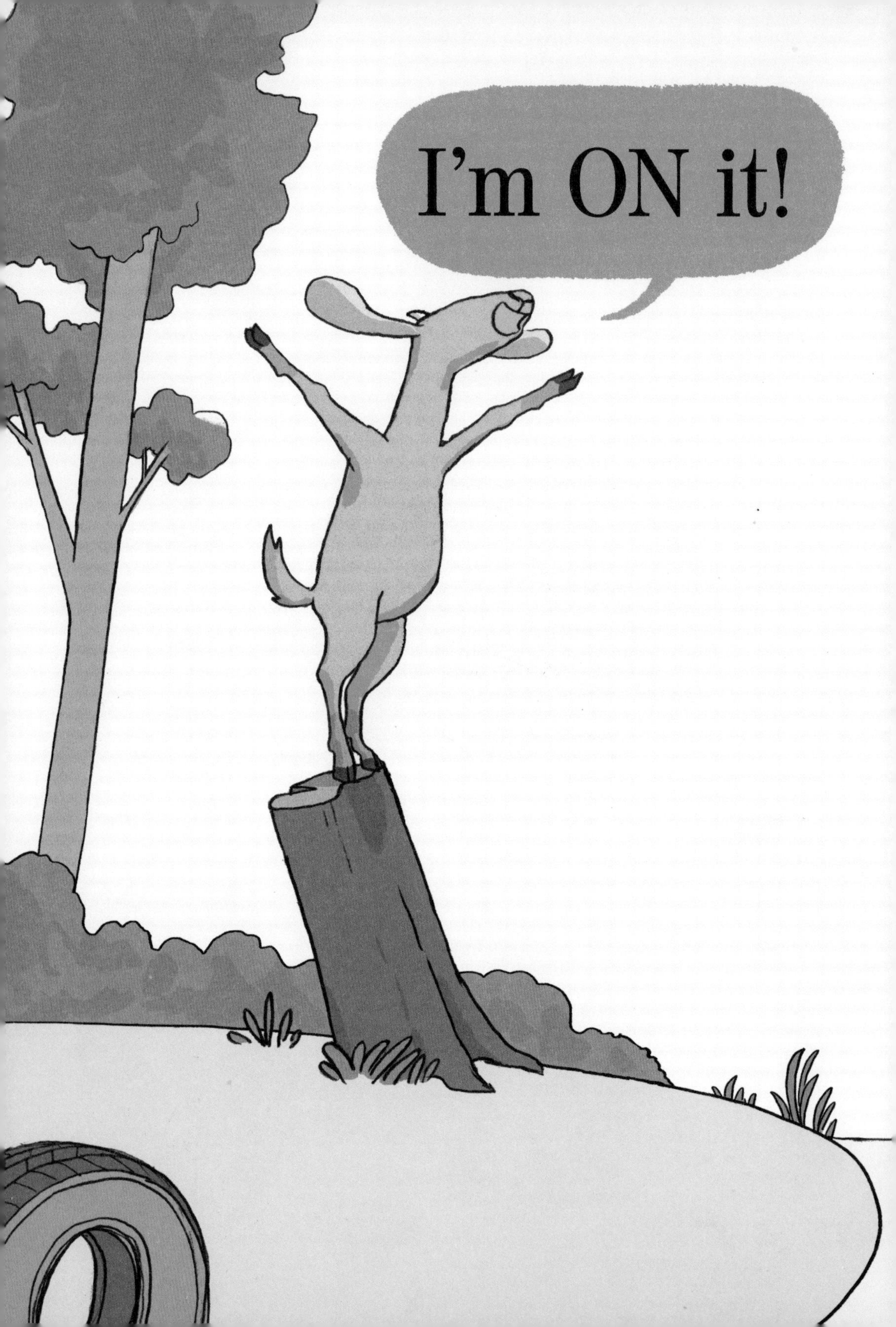
I'm ON it!

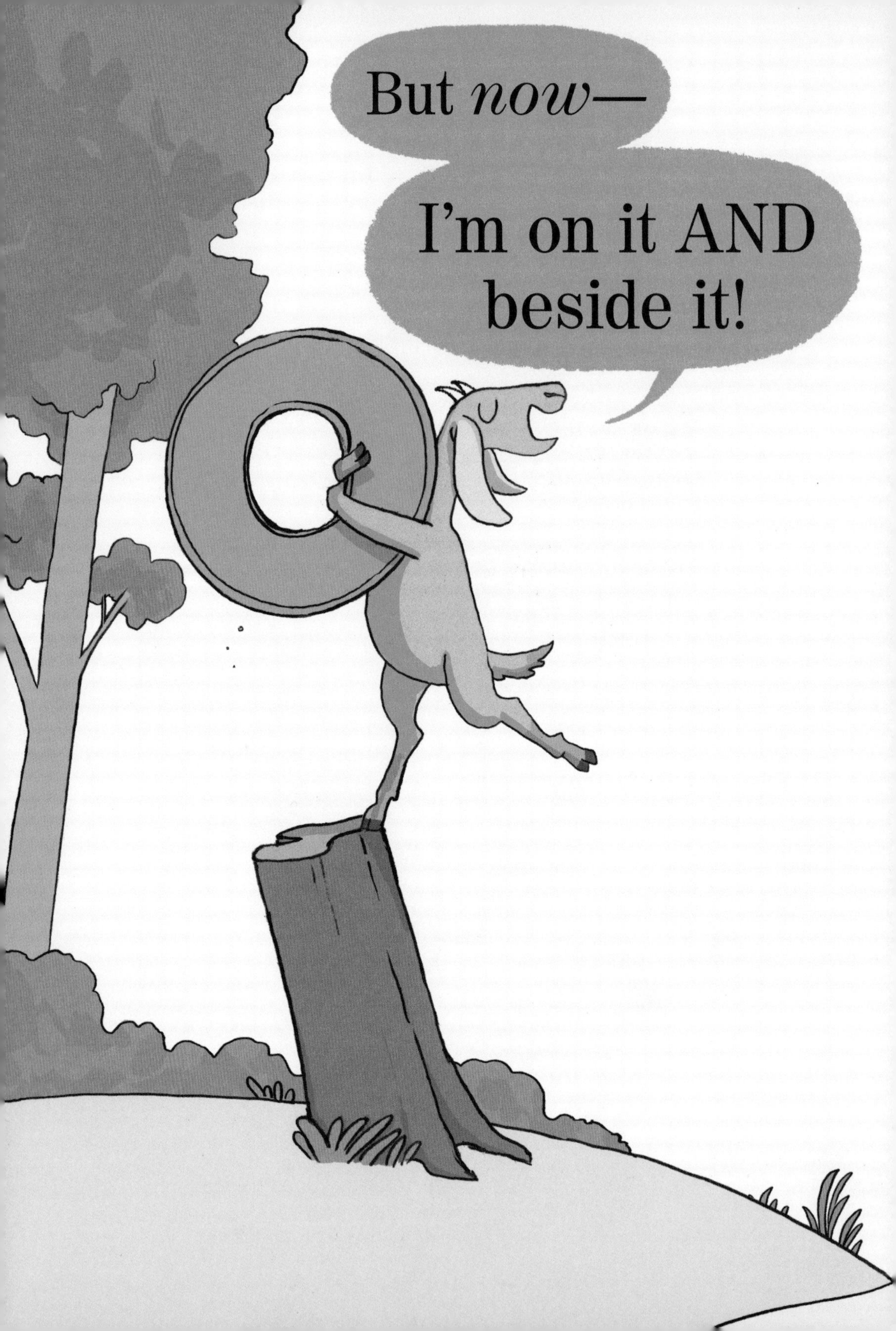
But *now*—
I'm on it AND beside it!

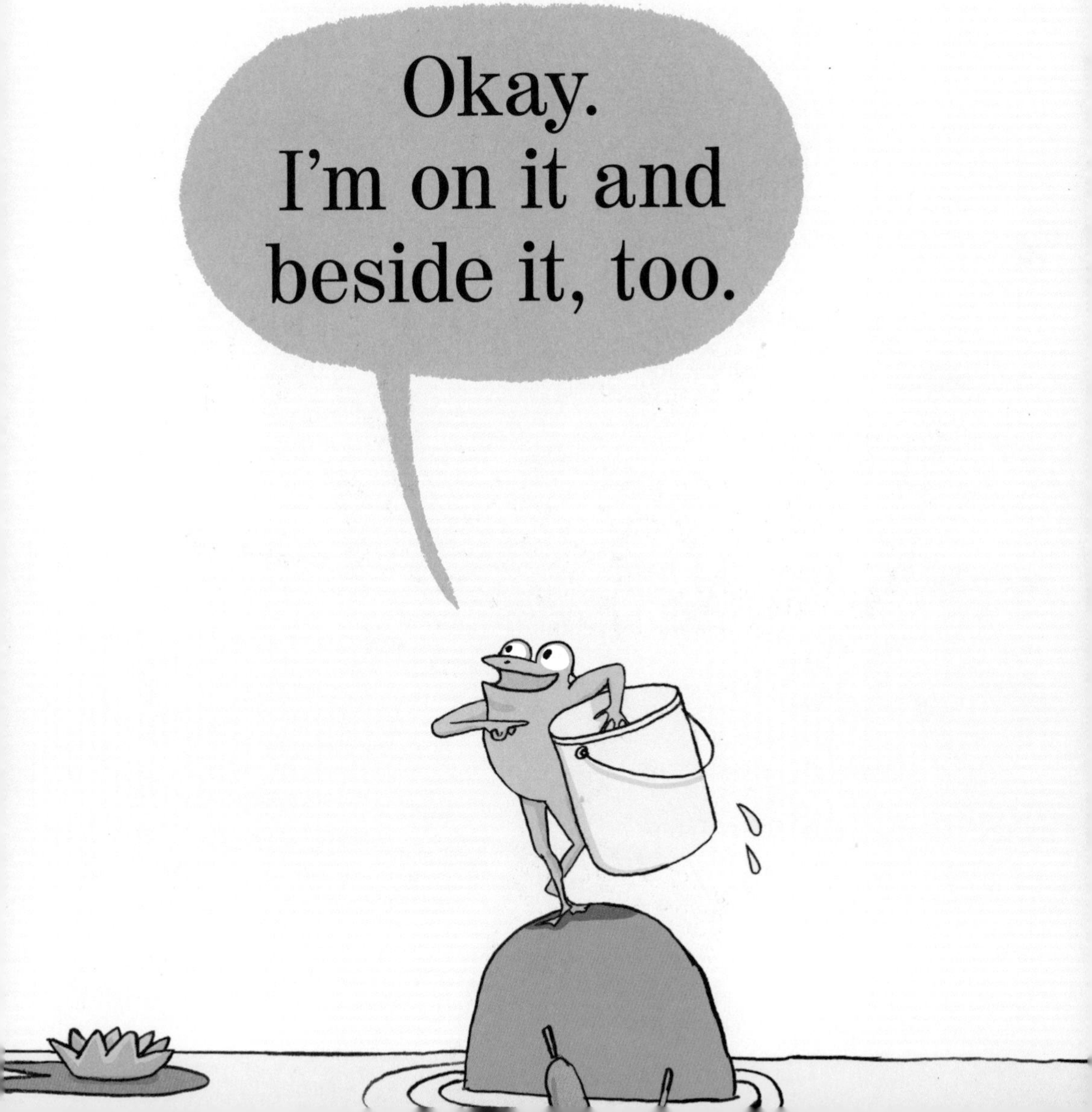
Okay.
I'm on it and
beside it, too.

Watch me! I'm on it, along it, above it, inside it, through it, and AROUND it!

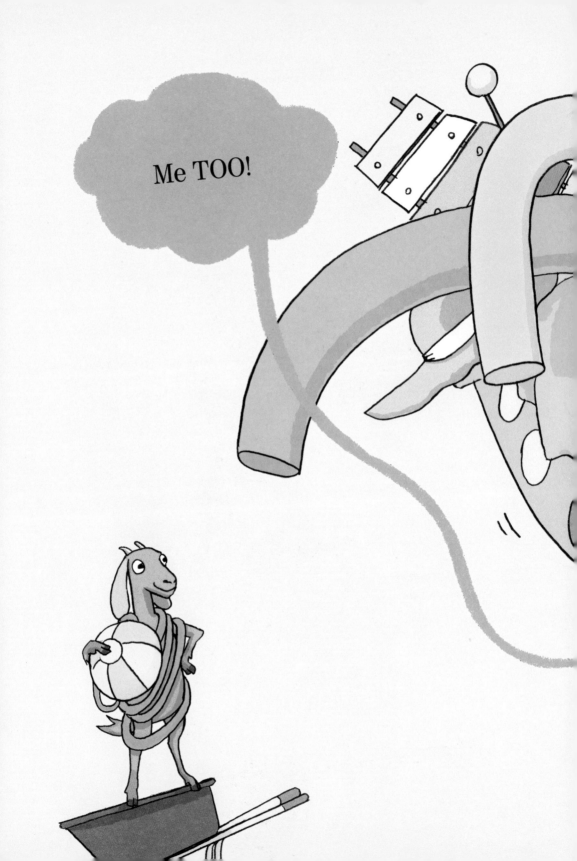

I am NEAR it.

And I am
far from it?

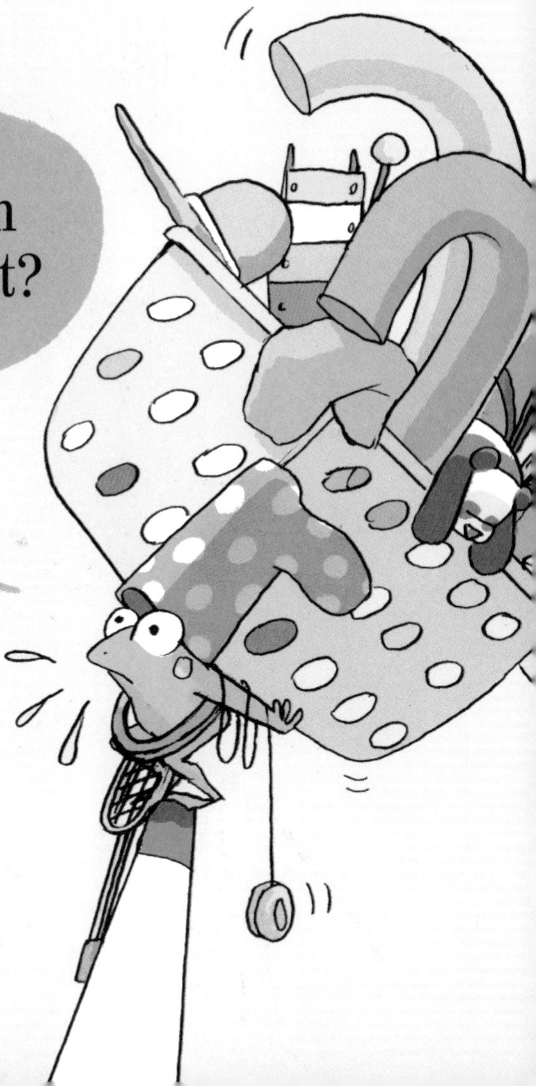

INTO THIS!

I am
SO—

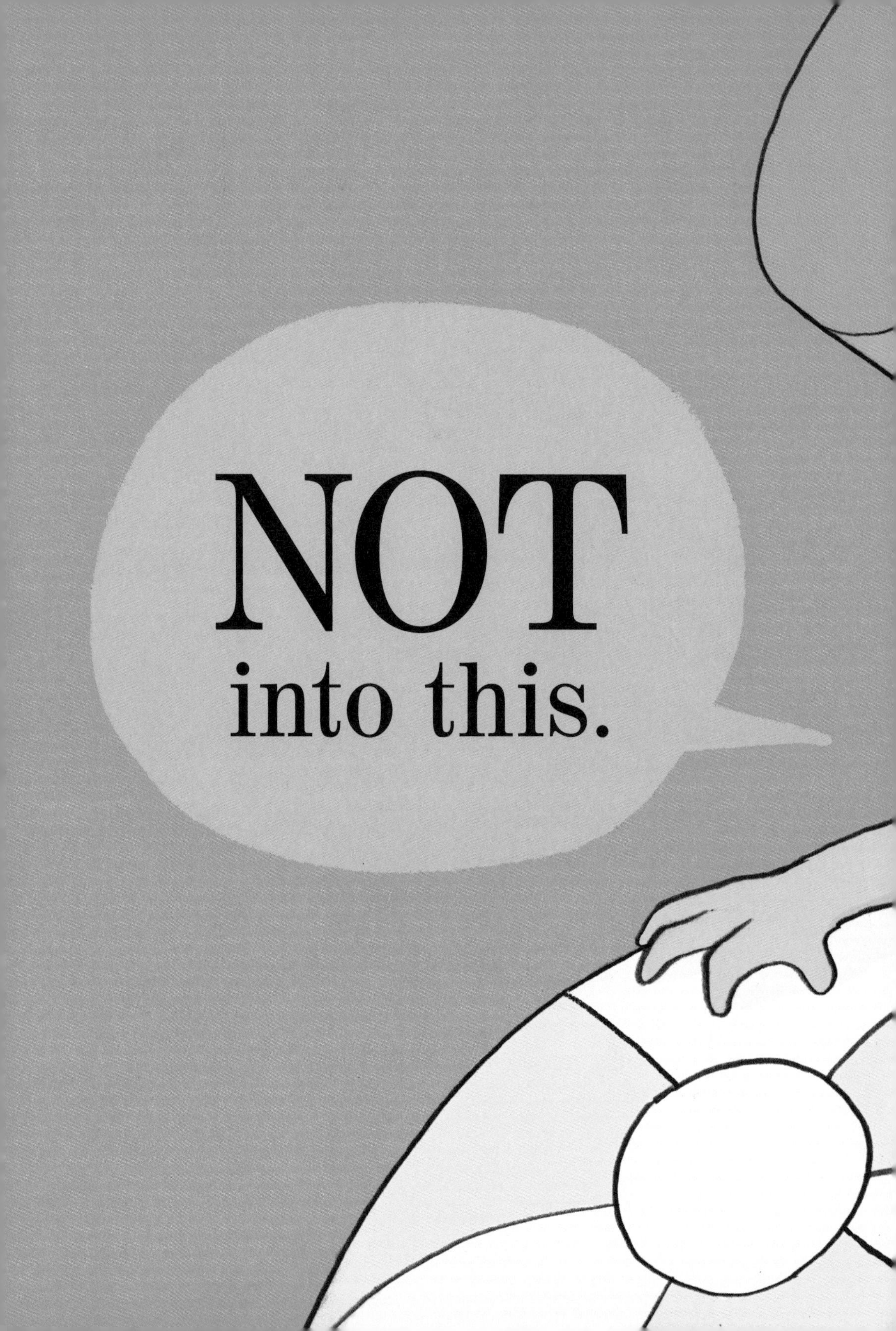
NOT
into this.

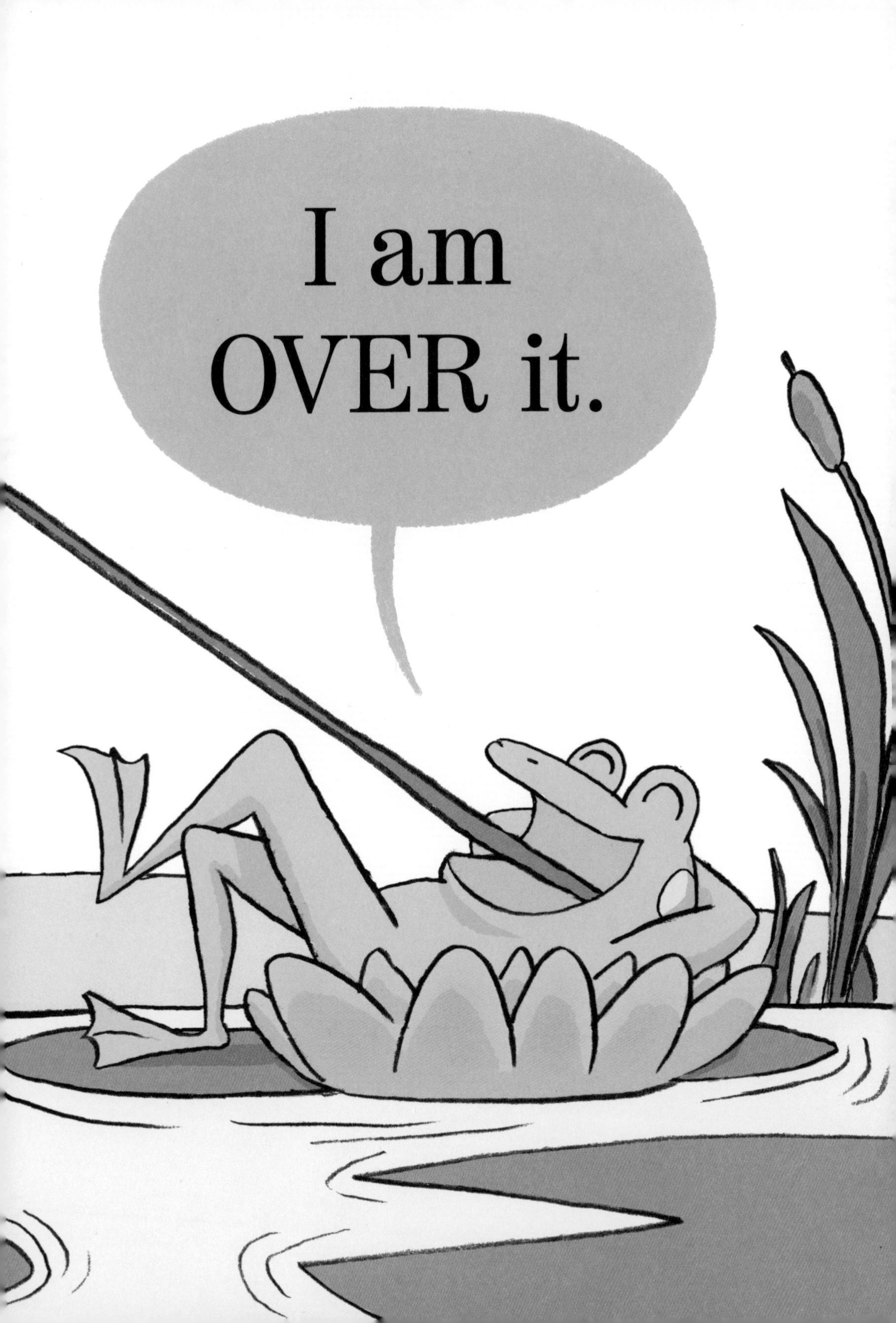
I am OVER it.

You know what?

For Casey Lurtz and Rachel Stern,
always with you

—AT

First Edition, May 2021 • 3 5 7 9 10 8 6 4 2 • FAC-034274-22157 • Printed in the United States of America

This book is set in Century 725/Monotype; Grilled Cheese BTN/Fontbros, with hand-lettering by Andrea Tsurumi.

Library of Congress Cataloging-in-Publication Data

Names: Tsurumi, Andrea, author, illustrator.
Title: I'm on it! / by [Mo Willems and] Andrea Tsurumi.
Other titles: I am on it!
Description: [New York : Hyperion Books for Children, 2021] | Series:
    Elephant & Piggie like reading! | Audience: Ages 4–8. | Audience: Grades 2–3. | Summary:
    "When Frog and Goat turn a simple game into an all-out competition, things get out of hand . . .
    until finally, they're over it"— Provided by publisher.
Identifiers: LCCN 2020026452 | ISBN 9781368066969 (hardback)
Subjects: CYAC: Games—Fiction. | Competition (Psychology)—Fiction.
    | Goats—Fiction. | Frogs—Fiction. | Humorous stories.
Classification: LCC PZ7.1.T783 Im 2021 | DDC [E]—dc23
LC record available at https://lccn.loc.gov/2020026452

Reinforced binding

Visit hyperionbooksforchildren.com
and pigeonpresents.com